Message in the Sky

Corey's Underground Railroad Diary

· Book Three ·

by Sharon Dennis Wyeth

Scholastic Inc. New York

Canada
1859

April 19, 1859

These past weeks have been very busy. Mama and Daddy and I made maple syrup. My friend Mingo was helping, too, now that he is part of the family. My family has made 200 gallons of syrup! From our very own maple trees!

Not too long ago, we didn't own any maple trees. In fact, we owned nothing at all. We were slaves on the Hart place in Kentucky. But we ran away to Canada on the Underground Railroad.

Now life could not be better. Mama says she has to pinch herself sometimes, she is so happy, especially now that we have built our

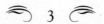

own cabin. And already, folks are calling her the best seamstress in Amherstburg!

As for myself, life is filled with things to do in every direction. Sometimes I even get too busy to write in my book. But today I am laid up in bed, so I can write all I want.

This afternoon I stepped on a nest of yellow jackets, and my toe is swollen, big as a melon!

Corey Birdsong (my signature)

Same Day, Later On

Now, I will practice my penmanship, like my teacher Mr. Alexander told me to.

Aa Bb Cc Dd
Corey — ten years old
Mingo — my old friend, might be fourteen
Angel — Mama
Roland — Daddy

Star — my baby sister
Hobbies — writing and birds

Even Later

My toe is still so swollen. Mama put witch hazel on it.

"Why did you go barefoot outdoors, Corey?" she scolded.

"I thought I heard a whistling swan fly by," I said. "I ran into the woods without my boots on."

Mingo worked at Thurman's rock quarry today after school. When he came home and saw my toe, his eyes popped like a frog's.

"No boot in this house will fit you now!" he said. "The cobbler will have to make a special size!"

That made me laugh. I am so glad that Mingo ran away from the Hart place in Kentucky like we did. He made it all the way to Amherstburg, Canada, all by himself. Now that he is living with us, he has taken our last name of Birdsong.

Evening

At supper, Star put her hands in the plate of fresh churned butter and wiped it in her hair. She is only a tot, but sometimes she can be naughty.

Daddy came home late from the blacksmith shop. When he saw my book out, he was pleased.

"Don't ever stop writing in your book, son," he said. "You are writing for all of us. Someday the Birdsong family will read your book and enjoy looking back on our lives."

April 21, 1859

After school today, Mingo and I helped Daddy clear the field. Daddy borrowed a horse from Mr. Foster's livery stable to help pull up the stumps. We are saving to buy our own horse, but first we must pay off our land. We are buying our place on time from Mr. Thurman.

My toe is fine. I think I had six stings on it! I will not go barefoot in the woods again.

April 22, 1859

Mr. Alexander has given me a dictionary. This way I can look up words when I am not sure how to spell them.

April 24, 1859

Today after church, we went next door to the Thurmans. Mr. and Mrs. Thurman and Gwen asked us to dinner. They also asked George and his family. Mama was happy to go visiting. She admires Mrs. Thurman's real china dishes.

Daddy talked to Mr. Thurman and Mr. Davis, George's father, about when to plant. Mr. Thurman and Mr. Davis said that we could put in some peas, but we should wait to plant the rest of our vegetables. Daddy said that was fine, since we still have to finish the clearing.

Clearing is hard work. Our field is filled with hundreds of big rocks. And every single one of those rocks, we have to dig up!

After dinner, Mingo and I played outdoors with Gwen and George. Gwen and Mingo played statues, while George and I climbed the elm tree. From the top of the tree, Gwen and Mingo looked odd. They twirled themselves around in the grass, then stopped as if they were frozen. Mingo landed on all fours and made a mule statue!

While George and I were in the tree, Gwen asked us to tie up her swing and we did.

When Mama came outdoors with Star, Gwen sat down in the swing with Star in her lap. Star liked swinging! She also likes Gwen, though she can't say her name. Instead of Gwen, Star calls her Den.

April 26, 1859

There are some pigeons living out back in the rocks. I see the same four every day. They are beautiful birds, and each one is different. I can hear them coo from the window.

April 27, 1859

Still clearing the field. We worked again after school today. Plenty of brush and stones and tree roots. We put the stones and the roots to the side for a fence.

April 28, 1859

Today in school, Mr. Alexander taught us how to write a letter. For homework, we have to write a letter to a friend in the class. I think I will write to George.

I will practice writing my letter to George in my diary. Then I will copy it onto another piece of paper.

April 28, 1859

Mr. George Davis
Amherstburg, Ontario, Canada

Dear George,

How about going swimming after school on Monday? We can go down to the river. Then you can come to my house, and I will show you our new chicks. Let me know if you want to go swimming.

Yours truly,
Corey Birdsong

April 29, 1859

When we got to school, Mr. Alexander had a letterbox. We dropped the letters we had written inside. This is somewhat like the town post office, where Mr. Peche is the postmaster.

When all the letters had been dropped in, Mr. Alexander asked Gwen to pass out the mail. George read the letter that I had written to him right then and there. He gave me a nod from across the room. That meant that he would come swimming on Monday.

April 30, 1859

This is the hardest I have ever worked in my life. Today, Mingo and I were digging out a stone in the middle of the field. It took hours to get that thing out of the ground! Then it was too heavy to carry. Daddy said that we have to plow around it. When winter comes, we'll slide it across the ice.

Same Day, Later On

This evening I called to the pigeons. I know that they were listening. The one with the pretty purple band on his wings stared right at me. He's got the scrawniest little legs! The dark one with the white tail feather paid me no mind. She was busy fluffing herself. The two spotted ones went off together, chasing something in the grass. Could have been a worm or maybe a cricket. The spotted ones are smaller than the other two, so maybe they are younger. They sure are fast!

May 2, 1859

After school, the river was cold! George and I went to the river. Swenson came along also. The river was too cold! George and I jumped in for only a minute and then ran out.

Swenson was splashing through the water like a hound, however. He must have ice in his blood. Else he was showing off!

I got a letter in school today. It was from Sammy Johnston. He was late getting his letter in. Some letter! He had drawn a picture of a heart with my name and Gwen's on it! I told him right then and there that I didn't like that. Gwen is not my girlfriend, I told him. She is my *friend*. A boy and a girl can be friends, if they feel like it! Sammy said that he was sorry. That the letter was only a joke.

George and Swenson did not come by the house after swimming. They had to go home to do chores.

May 3, 1859

After he came home from the blacksmith shop, Daddy began the plowing! Mr. Thurman has lent him a plow.

May 5, 1859

Put in peas. Mrs. Bentley came over and gave Mama some flower seeds. Mama is tickled. She has always wanted her own flower garden.

May 7, 1859

Mingo got paid at the rock quarry today. I wish I had me a paying job. But Mama and Daddy need my help at home, and I also have school work. Daddy says that Mingo can have a paying job if he wants to, because Mingo is almost a man. Besides, Mingo wants to help pay for his keep in our house. Daddy promised that when school is over, I can get me a job that pays.

May 9, 1859

Today Mr. Alexander asked Mingo about his homework. He still did not write his letter to put in the letterbox! Mingo is upset. He is the oldest in school, except on the days when Mama comes. Yet he is behind in reading and writing.

Same Day, Later On

This is a letter that Mingo wrote.

May 9, 1859

Mr. John Alexander
Schoolhouse
Amherstburg, Ontario, Canada

Dear Mr. Alexander,

Thank you for teaching me how to read and write. I am sorry that I am a slow learner. I could not learn to read at the place where I lived in Kentucky. On the Hart farm, ol' Hart, the owner, did not allow such things.

Before he left for Canada, Corey Birdsong did teach me my letters! Corey's father, Mr. Roland, taught Corey to read, against ol' Hart's wishes. Mr. Roland taught Corey on the sly.

On the Hart place in Kentucky, I lived with Aunt Queen. Aunt Queen was the one who raised me. When I ran away on the Underground Railroad, I had to leave Aunt Queen behind.

I wish that you could meet Aunt Queen. To me, she was the world's best person. She sang and told us stories.

Yours truly,
Mingo Birdsong

He has written a letter to Mr. Alexander. It is bold to write to the teacher. Maybe that is why Mingo was fretting so over this homework. He wanted that letter to be perfect because it was going to the teacher himself!

First Mingo wrote his letter in my book, and I helped him with the spelling. Then Mingo copied his letter on another piece of paper to take to school to put in the letterbox.

Even Later

I write this while everyone else is sleeping.

Helping Mingo write his letter made me think of the old days. Once Missus Susie, ol' Hart's wife, hit me in the face with her iron key. That was when I was waiting on the table and dropped the spoon. It hurt so much and my eye was bleeding. I don't like to remember that time.

But I do like remembering Aunt Queen! I remember how she told the tale of the "Tortoise and the Hare." The tortoise was slow, but in the end, she got where she was headed.

Aunt Queen was our friend. I miss her.

May 14, 1859

This morning I took some sewing into town for Mama. She has made some trousers for Mr. Bentley. Mr. Bentley is a very big man. (That's why they call him Malagasy Giant!) Mama made the trousers plenty roomy.

This afternoon, I split logs until dinnertime. Mama gave me a nickel! George and Swenson stopped by in the evening. I showed them the chicks. Then I showed them the pigeons. Swenson didn't seem too interested. But George did, especially when I called Scrawny and he flew right to me and perched himself on my shoulder! (Scrawny is the name I gave to the one with the purple band and scrawny little legs.)

May 16, 1859

Mr. Alexander wrote an answer to Mingo's letter! It went something like this —

Dear Mingo,

Thank you for your letter. You are
not a slow learner at all. You are a very
good student! Don't be shy about your
reading and writing. Your letter was
perfect! Not only that, you are at the
top of the class in arithmetic.

I am sorry to hear that you had to
leave a loved one in Kentucky. Aunt
Queen sounds like a wonderful person.
If you ever need anything, please ask me.

Yours truly,
Your teacher
John Alexander

Mingo said that he will keep Mr. Alexander's letter forever.

May 21, 1859

Today I called Scrawny again. He hopped onto my hand this time. I gave him some corn out of my pocket. Mingo was watching.

"You always did have a good way with birds, Corey," he said. "Remember the time in Kentucky when Aunt Queen gave you the name of Corey Birdsong? Before that day, you were just Corey."

"Aunt Queen gave me that name, Birdsong, because of all the bird calling I did back then," I said.

"When you did the whip-poor-will, Aunt Queen loved it," said Mingo. "And when you honked like a goose, she laughed."

Then Mingo wanted to call Scrawny himself. He held corn in his hand, but Scrawny did not come.

Same Day, Later On

I took Mama and Daddy out back to show them my pigeons.

"That one is Scrawny," I pointed out. "The dark one, I call Prissy. I haven't thought up names for the two little spotted ones."

Daddy grinned. He has always liked birds himself.

May 26, 1859

Star is walking! She walked across the floor of the cabin! She wasn't holding on to anyone's hands, and she didn't fall once! My whole family was there to see. We kissed my baby sister, one by one.

May 29, 1859

During church today, a family came in. Mr. Foster drove them here in his stagecoach. They are also from Kentucky. They are runaways! A father and two young sons who are the same size and who look very much alike. The family's name is Jenkins. Mr. Jenkins told us their story. It is sad. He and his two boys got across the lake to Canada, but they had to leave Mrs. Jenkins and a daughter behind. Seems that when they were running north, the family got separated. As soon as Mr. Jenkins gets settled, he wants to go back for his wife and daughter.

After Reverend Binga finished preaching, folks talked about how they could help the new family. Mr. and Mrs. Bentley offered them the little house next to the blacksmith shop to live in. The same one where my family lived before we got our own place!

Mama said that she was going to send some clothes that were too small for me for the boys, and that she would get to work making some new ones, too. Daddy said that he had clothes that would fit Mr. Jenkins. Mrs. Thurman said she has plenty of canned vegetables, and Mr. McCurdy offered to supply the family with bread. Other offers were made as well.

"Thank you. I had heard that people in Amherstburg were good folk," said Mr. Jenkins.

"Many of us have been in your shoes," Daddy spoke up. "We'll help you as best we can."

May 31, 1859

Today we planted 'taters. We worked until dark. My back was aching. Mama taught Star how to play pat-a-cake. She claps her hands, but she can't say the words.

June 1, 1859

After school today I went picking strawberries. Gwen and George came with me. First we picked over at the Davis place where George lives, and then we picked on the Thurman property. Last we picked on our place. Our pails were plenty full by the time we were done. My stomach was full also. I ate as many berries as I picked! I think that the ones growing on our place are the sweetest.

When we stopped to rest, George and I

played Duck on a Rock. Gwen had never heard of the game! I explained to her how to play.

"First we put a little stone on top of a big rock," I told her. "That little stone is the Duck."

"How can you say that is a duck," she asked, "when it's plain to see that it's a stone?"

"We just call it a duck," said George. "It's a game, don't you know?"

"Well, how do you play it?" asked Gwen.

"Everybody picks up a stone of their own and tries to knock the Duck off the rock," George answered.

"The one whose stone is farthest away from the Duck is the Duck," I said.

Gwen looked puzzled. But she picked a stone up off the ground. "Let me see if I can do it," she said.

Guess what? She took a throw and knocked the Duck off the rock on the first try!

"I won!" said Gwen.

Same Day, Later On

Forgot to write that I also found some pokeweed berries, for making more ink. Got a nice crow quill, too, for another pen.

June 2, 1859

Went with Mama to visit the new family. They seem settled in at the small house next door to the Bentleys. I found out something — the Jenkins boys are twins! One is named Just and the other one is Jim. I have never known twins before. They are little, but run faster than lightning. The clothes Mama gave them are a mite big, but she says she will take some tucks in them.

I went with Jim and Just next door to Mrs. Bentley's house. She gave us some milk and raisin pie! Then the twins and I went across to the blacksmith shop where Daddy was working with Mr. Bentley. Mr. Bentley and Daddy were working on a big anchor for one of the boats down at the Navy Yard. The forge was hot!

Mr. Jenkins was at the shop, too. He was watching. Daddy said that Mr. Jenkins has been helping folks around town. But soon he might be working for Mr. Thurman at the rock quarry.

June 4, 1859

We have been planting for two days. We put in beans. We put in corn. We put in tomatoes. We also planted carrots, beets, and rhubarb. Mama says there will be enough to feed us this winter, once she cans things. She has already made some strawberry jelly. I took three jars to the Davis place in exchange for milk from their cow.

I am too tired this evening. Too tired to even play with my birds. All I can do is lie in bed and listen to them.

June 5, 1859

After church, the Jenkins family came for dinner. Mr. Jenkins brought us a big bass he'd caught on the river. Mama buried it beneath the coals on the hearth and cooked it. We had custard made from our own eggs. The twins ate a lot for such little fellows.

After dinner, I showed off my pigeons. Just and Jim jumped up from the table and ran outside to see the pigeons.

"Coo-coo!" I called. Scrawny hopped up onto my shoulder.

"Coo-coo!" Prissy came and landed on my arm. Mr. Jenkins clapped, and the twins seemed amazed.

"Coo-coo! Coo-coo!" The two little spotted ones sailed over and sat on my head. That got the twins to giggling.

"Well done!" said Mr. Jenkins. "Those your birds?"

"They're just always around here," I explained. "They leave sometimes, but come back by evening."

"This must be their home place," he said. "No matter how many miles away they go, some birds always come back to their home."

"How can they find their home, when they fly far away?" asked Mingo.

"They got good memories, I expect," said Mr. Jenkins.

June 6, 1859

Today I cleared a spot next to the house for Mama's flower garden.

June 9, 1859

The peas are coming up!

June 10, 1859

Mingo was talking to Mr. Jenkins in the rock quarry. Mr. Jenkins is working there now. He told Mingo that he plans to buy his wife's and daughter's freedom. He has heard that they were caught and are living as slaves in Kentucky. He is going to work as hard as he can and save the money. When he has enough, he will find a way of sending the money South for his wife's and daughter's purchase.

"It might take a long, long time," he told Mingo. "But I am determined to do it."

Now Mingo has the idea that he wants to save his money, too! He wants to buy freedom for Aunt Queen! I promised Mingo that I would help him.

June 12, 1859

After church today Mrs. Bentley spoke to some of the folks about the Jenkins family. She is worried that the boys have no mother. So, she is starting a freedom fund for the family. She has asked that folks give what they can. The fund will help Mr. Jenkins buy his wife and daughter! Mama and Daddy said that they would give what they could. We all want Just and Jim to have their mother and sister back.

Same Day, Later On

I told Daddy and Mama that Mingo plans to buy Aunt Queen's freedom. Mingo had not told them.

"Can folks help Mingo buy Aunt Queen, too?" I asked.

"We can't ask folks to do more than they are able to," Daddy said quietly. "Mrs. Bentley has started a freedom fund for the Jenkins. We can't start another one."

"I'm saving my money for Aunt Queen," Mingo said stubbornly. "Aunt Queen is my family."

"I'll help pay for Aunt Queen, too," I vowed, "when I get a job. Maybe our family can put money aside for the Jenkins family and for Aunt Queen."

"We can put by a little," said Daddy. "But we still have the farm to pay off, and tools to buy, and a horse and a cow."

"Aunt Queen is more important than a cow!" Mingo said. He looked as if he might cry.

Mama wiped the corner of her eye with her

apron. "Aunt Queen is old. I hate to think of her dying a slave."

"We'll do what we can," promised Daddy.

June 13, 1859

Mingo wants to write a letter to ol' Hart. I told Daddy about it. Daddy said that we would write a letter together. That way we will know how much money we need in order to buy Aunt Queen's freedom.

June 14, 1859

This is what we said in the letter to ol' Hart.

Dear Mr. Hart,

We are writing about Queen. She has been a friend to us and like a mother. Since she is getting on in her years, we thought you might not mind selling her. If so, please write back with the purchase price. Once we pay for her freedom, we will get a friend to bring her to us.

Please write back in care of Postmaster Peche, Amherstburg, Ontario, Canada.

Yours truly,
Roland Birdsong
Angel Birdsong
Corey Birdsong
Mingo Birdsong

June 15, 1859

After school today, Mingo and I took the letter to Postmaster Peche. My hand was shaking when I gave that letter over to be mailed. Our letter will go the Hart farm in Kentucky.

When ol' Hart opens the letter, he will know for sure that we've settled in the town of Amherstburg.

He will know that after Mingo ran away, he settled here, too, to be with us.

When I mailed the letter, I felt scared.

Mingo told me not to worry.

"Ol' Hart gave up on us being his slaves again," said Mingo. "Didn't he try to chase us down with slave catchers and dogs? But we all came through to freedom. First your daddy, then you and your mama and Star, then lastly me. We are safe, as long as we are in Canada."

June 16, 1859

Mama and Daddy said that I could get a job. School is almost over, and I want to put some money aside for Aunt Queen's purchase.

I thought of names for my other two little pigeons! I will call them Just and Jim, just like the Jenkins boys! That's because the littlest pigeons are so very fast.

June 17, 1859

Plants are sprouting up all over the garden! Mama has got her flowers in. Mingo and I made a scarecrow. I played with my pigeons. They come whenever I want them to. They follow me everywhere! It helps when I have corn in my hand.

Same Day, Later On

I got five wrong on my arithmetic test. 5 X 8 = 40! I said it equals 45. That was a stupid mistake!

June 18, 1859

Mama asked me to walk with her to town. She had some sewing to deliver to Mrs. McCurdy. I carried Star on my shoulders. Though Star can walk, she gets tired when she has to walk too far. On the way we saw lots of robins and purple martins.

Mama delivered a white muslin shirt and a white baker's apron for Mr. McCurdy. Mama also made an apron for Mrs. McCurdy and a white blouse with ruffles. McCurdy's Bakery smelled good! Mrs. McCurdy gave me a scone, and she also gave one to Star. She filled

Mama's basket with bread. She seemed pleased with the sewing that Mama had done for her.

"You'll have your family's bread for the next two months, Mrs. Birdsong," said Mrs. McCurdy.

Mama said that was too much for Mrs. McCurdy to pay her.

"Your work is fine and worth a whole lot more," said Mrs. McCurdy. Then she gave Mama the rest of the white muslin cloth to take home!

On the way home, we went down to the water and Star fed her scone to the gulls.

June 20, 1859

Mr. Alexander told us that we would not have another spelling bee this year. Instead we will have a contest for the best oration. Oration is a word I did not know before. Mr. Alexander wrote it on the board and I copied it. It means that we are going to all give speeches. But before we give our speeches, we have to write them.

The subject of our orations will be "What Does Freedom Mean?"

June 21, 1859

I have a job! After school I went to the river and saw the captain of the *Pearl*. I asked if he knew of a job. The captain said that as a matter of fact, he was looking for someone to swab the deck when he comes into port. He said that he could also use someone to take packages off. I said that I could do it! I cannot believe how lucky I am! I have always liked the captain, and the *Pearl* is a very fine ferryboat.

June 22, 1859

Mama said that I could help the captain out, but only when the *Pearl* is in the harbor. She does not want me going across the river to Michigan and certainly never across the lake to Ohio. She is still worried about slave catchers. Now that so many are running away from slavery, there are more slave catchers than ever. If they catch a runaway slave, the catchers can get the reward money.

June 23, 1859

"What Does Freedom Mean?" by Corey Birdsong.

Freedom is being with your family on your own place. Freedom is not to be hit in the face with an iron key. Freedom is making your own sweet maple syrup from your own maple trees.

Freedom is making many more friends, like my family has in Amherstburg.

June 24, 1859

I went to work on the *Pearl* today. Swabbed the deck while the ferryboat was in the harbor. I heard the captain talking abolitionist talk with the town crier. They got to talking about John Brown. Mr. Osborne, one of our friends in town, is in the States with John Brown now! Folks say he is doing abolitionist work, but no one has heard from him.

June 25, 1859

This is Mingo's composition for the oration contest. I helped him with the spelling.

"What Does Freedom Mean?" by Mingo Birdsong.

I am free, but not free as a bird. A bird can fly over the water.

I am free, but not free as a star. A star shines bright for all to see, but I cannot be seen by all. If I were back in the States, I would have to hide.

The stars that shine in Canada are the same stars that shine in Kentucky. When I look at the sky at night, Aunt Queen is looking up, too. Yet I am free and she is not. I want to look at the sky with Aunt Queen, together, in whatever spot we please.

The stars in the sky are for all. So is freedom.

Same Day, Later On

I told Mingo that I like his composition. Daddy read it also. And then Mingo read it out loud to Mama. I read mine, too.

"What good writers my two boys are," said Mama. "I am proud of you both."

Then she gave each of us a new white shirt.

June 27, 1859

So much has happened. Ol' Hart sent us a letter! Also, it is the last day of school and Mingo won the oration contest. Mr. Alexander gave Mingo a certificate with his name on it. The certificate says, "Best Orator, Amherstburg Schoolhouse."

Same Day, Later On

This is the way ol' Hart's letter went:

To Roland, Angel, Corey, and Mingo,

I reckon you can take Queen if you want. She isn't much use with her poor legs, anyhow. I'll give her to you for $100.

Send somebody down with the money and I'll give Queen to 'em.

Master Robert Hart

Same Day, Later On

Mingo is so happy. As soon as we save enough money, he will get to see Aunt Queen. Not only that, he won the oration contest. To top it off, he has learned to call the pigeons. He cooed to Scrawny, Prissy, Just, and Jim, and each one of them came to him! I was surprised.

"I've been practicing," he said.

June 28, 1859

Mingo and I built a crate for the pigeons. The crate has a handle for carrying.

Daddy gave us an idea about a pigeon race! Maybe George, Gwen, and Swenson can come over and see.

Same Day, Later On

We put Just and Jim (the pigeons!) in the new crate so that they could try it out. They seemed to like it. Something odd — we can't find Scrawny and Prissy.

June 29, 1859

Today I worked on the *Pearl*. Then Mingo and I had our pigeon race. First we put Just and

Jim in the case. Then I took them to the middle of the woods and let them free.

"Fly home fast, boys!" I told them. I watched them sail into the sky. Then I ran home myself. Mingo was there waiting, and so were the pigeons! I was so excited. The birds had flown straight home.

"Who won the race?" I asked Mingo.

"Just came home first," said Mingo. "Jim came in second. Of course, the third pigeon was really a slowpoke."

"What third pigeon?" I asked, looking around.

Mingo laughed. "You! Just and Jim came in twenty minutes ago. I began to think that you'd gotten lost."

June 30, 1859

Had another pigeon race. This time George, Gwen, and Swenson were over. Mingo, George, and Swenson took Just and Jim out to the woods this time. It took them a while. Mingo said that he wanted to take the birds out a good five miles. Gwen and I waited almost an hour, but then we saw the birds coming. Just won again!

While Gwen and I were waiting for Mingo, George, and Swenson to come back, we found Scrawny and Prissy. They've made a nest in some rocks farther away from the house. The nest has two eggs! Guess I won't bother them with racing for a while.

Gwen dug up some sassafras roots for Mama. Mama is going to dye the rest of the white cloth for curtains. The curtains will be pale pink.

July 3, 1859

The captain asked if I could go on a boat ride with him tomorrow. He needs an extra hand to cross the river with him to Michigan.

If I ask Mama, it will only worry her. Mingo thinks that it's fine that I go. It has been a long time now, since ol' Hart put the reward signs out for me. And now I look completely different, because I have grown. Besides, when we get to the Michigan side, I will stay in the boat.

I am looking forward to my boat ride!

July 4, 1859

Today was a pretty day for a boat ride! A big cloud was in the sky, and it seemed to be following us. After I brought the packages up out of the hold, I went back down and waited. On shore there seemed to be a celebration, probably for Independence Day. I would have liked to explore. It has been a long time since I've seen the States. I felt strange. The United States is where I was born, but I dared not get off the boat.

One of the sailors hung out a fishing line and caught a big trout.

I put twenty-five cents in the hidey-hole for Aunt Queen's freedom.

July 5, 1859

Today I had a great idea! I took Just and Jim on the *Pearl* in their crate! I let them fly home from the harbor. Mingo was there waiting. This time Jim came in first!

I wonder if Just and Jim could find their way home if I took them all the way to Michigan.

July 9, 1859

The captain asked me to go to Michigan again. I took Just and Jim with me. I did not let them out of their crate until the ferryboat docked on the other side. When I got home, they were there waiting. Mingo had to work at the quarry, so I don't know which bird came in first. But what does it matter? They made it home, all the way from Michigan!

Next week, the captain is going to take a trip across the lake to Ohio. If I go with him, he will pay me a dollar! Mama would be worried, so I won't tell her. I plan to take Just and Jim with me. I will let them out of their crate in Ohio.

July 10, 1859

After church I told George and Swenson about my plan to take the pigeons to Ohio.

George was very excited. But that mulish Swenson doesn't believe that Just and Jim could find their way home.

"How will we know if you let the pigeons out in the States?" said Swenson. "You could let them out while you're still on the lake."

"You will have to take my word for it," I told him.

Swenson makes me mad.

July 11, 1859

Mingo is working hard every day. Also, Daddy did a big job down at the Navy Yard. Mama is planning to sell her strawberry jam at the Emancipation Day celebration in August. She is also making some lace to sell. But I think it will be a very long time before our family can save $100.

Same Day, Later On

Scrawny and Prissy had their babies! I took Star to see them in their nest.

July 12, 1859

Today I took Just to the woods and before I let him go I tied a message to one of his feathers. When the pigeon came home, Mingo saw that the message was still there.

I'll do the same thing when I go to Ohio! I will tie something to Jim's and Just's tails to prove that they were there. Mingo will be watching for the pigeons when they come home. Then he will go and get Swenson. Swenson will see that my pigeons are smart and fast!

I did not tell Mingo everything, however. I

did not tell him that in order for my plan to work, I will have to get off the boat.

July 21, 1859

I am writing this at dawn. Leaving on the *Pearl* this morning.

Today I will make more money for Aunt Queen's freedom fund.

Same Day, Later On
Sandusky, Ohio

I am in a fix! I don't know what to do! I got off the boat and —

July 22, 1859

So much has happened. I am in hiding. I am with a girl named Gladys and her mother. Gladys's mother is sick. We are hiding in a cave behind a waterfall. The waterfall is beneath a bridge. Yesterday, I heard footsteps on the bridge up above us. I was so frightened that I spilled my ink. Just is with me in his crate. But Jim is gone. I let him fly away when I got off the *Pearl* in Ohio. I was going ahead with my plan to prove that the pigeons had made it all the way to Ohio. But I didn't count on being left by the boat. More later.

Same Day, Later On

Gladys's mother is so very sick. She shivers with cold, yet her head feels very hot. Gladys puts wet cloths on her mother's head to bring down the fever. Though I am sorry that the *Pearl* left without me, I am not sorry that I went with Gladys when she asked me to follow her. I was tying the message to Jim's tail feather when Gladys saw me down at the dock.

Same Day, Later On

I walked to the town. We are so close to the dock! Yet the cave is completely hidden. No sign of the *Pearl.* But I did find an apothecary. I asked the pharmacist for medicine for a person with chills and a burning up fever. He gave me some powders of something called quinine. Luckily, the captain had paid me, so I could buy the medicine. I also stopped at the bakery to buy some bread for the three of us. Gladys and her mother have been living off berries.

I cannot believe that I am walking the

streets of Ohio. I feel nervous. Gladys and her mother are runaways. The slave catchers are after them. Maybe they will catch me, too, and send me back to Kentucky, far away from my family. I must try to be brave.

July 23, 1859

The powders from the apothecary have helped! Gladys's mother seems to be better. But she is very thirsty. Gladys and I take turns climbing around to the creek to bring back water. Gladys has a cup and I have my canteen. Gladys's mother asked me how I got here. I told her that I was tying a scrap of newspaper to the tail of one of my pigeons to prove that he had been in Ohio. That was when her daughter tapped me on the shoulder and asked me to follow her.

Gladys's mother smiled, but she seemed

confused. Then she asked me to take Gladys back home with me! She wants Gladys to get to Canada. But Gladys says she cannot leave her mother!

Of course, I have no idea how I will get home myself! Mama and Daddy are probably so worried.

I still have Just in his crate. I have found him lots of bugs.

Why do I keep writing? What good will it do?

Same Day, Later On

I have drawn a map on a piece of paper from my book. It shows the dock, it shows the road where I walked with Gladys to get to the waterfall. It shows the cave behind the waterfall and the bridge above it. Then I signed my name. I rolled the piece of paper up until it was very small. Gladys asked me what I was doing.

"I will tie this message to my pigeon's tail feather," I explained. "My friend Mingo will find it when the pigeon flies home. My father will come and get us. I am sure of that."

"What if the message falls off?" Gladys asked. "What if it rains and the message gets wet?"

I did not know what to say.

Gladys went outside and came back with a quill feather. "Put the message inside this," she said. I rolled the paper even smaller and stuffed it into the quill. Then I tied the feather onto my bird's tail.

"Fly home, Just!" I said, letting the pigeon go free. Gladys and I watched the bird sail through the sky.

"What if your pigeon doesn't make it to Canada?" Gladys asked.

"I will keep going to the dock and wait for the *Pearl*," I explained.

I am acting brave for Gladys. I hope that

Just makes it home! The captain must have discovered that I got off the boat as soon as he got back to Amherstburg. If only someone would come to find me!

July 24, 1859

I wanted to walk to the dock, but there were footsteps on the bridge. We also heard horses galloping by. And worst of all, we heard dogs! The slave catchers are out looking for someone.

Gladys's mother is burning with fever again.

I crawled out at dusk and got very lucky. I found a rabbit caught in somebody's trap. We have been so hungry!

Same Day, Later On

Gladys's mother is tossing and turning. She has asked me again to leave her behind and take Gladys to Canada. She has already lost her husband and two little boys. She wants her daughter to get to freedom. But Gladys will not leave. I am very scared. Tomorrow, I will have to venture out.

"We will all get to Canada," I promised.

July 25, 1859

I write this at dawn. Gladys and I were up all night. There were noises on the bridge. The most surprising thing has happened. Gladys is Mr. Jenkins's daughter! Gladys's mother is Mrs. Jenkins. I found this out when Gladys and I were talking about the pigeons.

"I heard you call your pigeon Just," she told

me. "I had a little brother whose name is Just. He has a twin named Jim. Mother and I do not know what became of them."

I almost leapt out of my skin I was so surprised. "They are free and living in Canada with your father," I told her.

Gladys was so happy! She tried to wake her mother to tell her.

More than ever, I must reach Canada with Gladys and her mother! I am venturing out of the cave.

July 26, 1859

The story has a happy ending. When I was walking to town on the road, who should I see coming my way but Roland Birdsong? Daddy had come to get me with the captain of the *Pearl!* They were in a wagon. I almost didn't see them, since I was trying to make myself scarce on the road. But then Daddy called out to me. I was never so glad to see him in my life!

I took them to the cave. Daddy and the captain carried Mrs. Jenkins out of the cave and up the creek bank. They laid her in the wagon and covered her with a blanket. Gladys and I hopped in beside her. The *Pearl* was at the dock waiting.

When we got home to Amherstburg, Mama was so glad to see me that she forgot to scold me for leaving the harbor on the *Pearl*. Mr. Jenkins was shocked to see his daughter and wife. Just and Jim hung on to their mother. She smiled and kissed them. Mrs. Jenkins is still very sick. Mrs. Bentley is taking care of her. Also, Reverend Binga has sent the doctor to the Jenkins house.

August 8, 1959

Mrs. Jenkins has died. She held on for quite a bit, but in the end she was too weak to be saved. Today is the Emancipation Day celebration. It will not be the same as last year's. We will have Mrs. Jenkins's funeral.

Same Day, Later On

I saw Gladys at the funeral. She was trying to be brave. Reverend Binga preached a good sermon, Daddy said.

"She is at peace," said Reverend Binga. "Before she died, she knew freedom. Before she left us, she knew that her sons and her daughter and her husband would have a free life."

Everyone was at the funeral. Just and Jim sat very still next to their father.

Mrs. Binga asked Mama to sing with the choir. They sang "Michael, Row the Boat Ashore."

August 9, 1859

Mingo told me what happened when I got left in Ohio. He said that Jim made it home, but he had lost his message. When Daddy talked with the captain of the *Pearl*, he and Mama figured out what must have happened. The *Pearl* came back over for me, but I was nowhere to be found. Later when Just flew home, his message was still on him. So Daddy and the captain came to find me.

This evening I sat with my pigeons. Scrawny and Prissy have moved closer to the house again with their two little ones. Mama's flowers are blooming. I am happy to be home, but Mrs. Jenkins's death has left me sad.

August 14, 1859

Gladys was at church. She was sitting with Gwen. Swenson was there, too. He was nice. He said that there is talk in town that I am a conductor on the Underground Railroad. I told him that I am not a conductor, that I was only helping out Gladys and her mother. George said that I am too a conductor. Didn't I help two people find their freedom?

August 25, 1859

I have been too busy to write. We are picking the crops. Potatoes, carrots, beans, melons, tomatoes, corn! And I am also helping Revered Binga pick his apples.

Mama is canning all day long.

Last night Mingo ate fourteen ears of corn!

September 5, 1859

Today Mingo and I took a bushel of beans and some tomatoes to Mrs. Bentley's. Mrs. Bentley sent us back home with two bushels of squash. But first she gave Mingo and me some rhubarb pie. I hated the bitter taste, but I did not let on.

September 14, 1859

Still harvesting! Daddy is so pleased. Tonight we ate chicken.

I said "hey" to Gladys today. She was at the Thurman house. She and Gwen were playing jackstones with some stones and a wooden ball. Gwen said that she is going to teach Gladys to play Duck on a Rock. Then the girls will play against the boys.

September 18, 1859

We had the Jenkins family to dinner today. Jim and Just and Gwen played with the pigeons. After dinner, Mr. Jenkins said that he wanted to speak to us. What he had to say was a surprise. He is giving us his freedom fund for Aunt Queen's purchase. Mingo grinned from ear to ear. Folks at the church had wanted Mr. Jenkins to use that money to find a bigger house to live in.

"That money was raised for freedom," Mr. Jenkins explained to us. "I'll make the money in time to set up my house. You all should use that money to bring home your Aunt Queen."

September 21, 1859

We wrote a letter to ol' Hart. It went this way.

Dear Mr. Hart,

We have the money to purchase Queen. Please let us know when we can send a friend to pay you and to fetch Queen. Write in care of Postmaster Peche in Amherstburg, Ontario, Canada.

Yours truly,

The Birdsong family

September 24, 1859

Today Gwen and Gladys came over. While Mama was canning, they watched Star. I was out in the garden digging potatoes with Mingo. When Mingo and I came indoors, we heard Gladys singing. She was singing "Twinkle, Twinkle, Little Star" to my sister. Star liked that song. Maybe because her name is in it!

October 1, 1859

These are some of the words that Star can say!

Mama	milk
Dada	bread
bird	hot

doll

bed

'tater

corn

fire

flower

blanket

chair

cold

hungry

sleepy

Mingo

Gwen

Gladys

Corey!

At last my baby sister can say my name. She does not call me Dorey anymore.

October 2, 1859

I woke up and my pigeons were gone. Could it be that it got too cold for them?

"They know their way home," Daddy said. "They'll be back when they're ready."

October 5, 1859

School has started. Right off, I am having problems with arithmetic. I have forgotten my times tables, yet Mingo knows his perfectly. Mingo is trying to help me.

"If I ate seven ears of corn for breakfast, seven for lunch, and seven for dinner, what would that mean?" he asked me.

"That would mean that you are sick to your stomach," I joked.

"No, really," said Mingo, "what is the answer?"

"Twenty-one ears of corn," I told him.

"Very good, Corey," he said. "Was that so hard?"

Same Day

In school we are studying geography. Mr. Alexander showed us the globe. The world is a mighty big place! Someone in our town has gone to study in Scotland! Once the only place I knew was Kentucky. But then I went to Ohio and Michigan. Now here I am in Amherstburg.

October 9, 1859

The maple trees have all turned colors, and now the leaves are falling off. Mama says that they are like a big colorful carpet. Today something wonderful happened. My bird Swan came back to the woods next to the house! He lived down by the creek all winter. Now he has come back this year.

I can't wait until the spring when Just and Jim, Scrawny, Prissy, and their babies come back. I miss my pigeons!

October 14, 1859

Tomorrow there is a social at church. Everyone is excited. Mama made a gingham dress for Gladys. All that Gladys and Gwen can talk about is dancing. I will not be dancing at some social, not me! George and Swenson say they won't dance either. Mingo said that he might give it a try.

October 15, 1859

The social was fun. George and I entered a three-legged race. We came in second. The Jenkins twins, Just and Jim, came in first!

There was a mighty fine fiddler at the social from Chatham. There was also drumming. And Mingo had me doing my birdcalls. When I honked like a goose, Gladys laughed.

October 18, 1859

At last a letter has come from ol' Hart! It goes like this:

To Roland and Angel,

Mrs. Hart and I will let Queen go for the price of $125. Send somebody to fetch her in the first part of November. The price has gone up to $125 because I had to pay a doctor to look at Queen's legs.

Master Hart

October 20, 1859

We are learning division in school. I did well on my test. I only got two wrong. Mingo got his test perfect.

Today in geography we were studying our continents. Mr. Alexander told us about South America. Then on the globe, he showed us the continent of Africa.

"Our people came from Africa," he said.

I was confused, because I was born in Kentucky.

"Your ancestors were born in Africa," Mr. Alexander explained. Then I remembered that Mama's grandmother had been born there. Mama's grandmother was my great-grandmother. My ancestor who was born in Africa!

October 22, 1859

Cold weather has set in. Mama got out our winter coats and mufflers.

October 25, 1859

We have heard the news that John Brown is in jail! He was leading some of his men at a place called Harpers Ferry. Some say that John Brown is a madman. But I heard the captain of the *Pearl* say that John Brown is a freedom fighter.

Our friend Mr. Osborne was with John Brown. I wonder what happened to him.

November 1, 1859

We have given Reverend Binga the freedom fund. He has gone to fetch Aunt Queen!

November 3, 1859

A snowstorm has left ice on the field. Mingo and I went skating. Then we took the sled out. We loaded it up with the stones that we found too heavy to move last spring. With the sled, it was not hard to slide the stones across the ice and out of the field. Those big stones will be good for the fence. Daddy calls the sled our "stone boat."

November 15, 1859

On the day Aunt Queen came, big white flakes fell from the sky like feathers. Mingo was at the woodpile, splitting logs. Daddy was on the roof, patching. I was cleaning the chicken house. We heard the bells on Reverend Binga's horse-drawn sleigh.

"She's here!" Mingo cried.

I ran to see. Mama came out of the house, holding Star's hand. Daddy climbed down off the roof.

There sat Aunt Queen wrapped up in a quilt, next to Reverend Binga.

What a celebration we had that evening! So many folks came by, even in the cold weather. We kept a lamp lit in the window. The Thurmans came to say hello, and the Bentleys, and the Jenkinses. The McCurdys came with fresh rolls.

Aunt Queen was so wrapped up in quilts on the trip that she didn't even get cold. When she hugged us, she felt warm as an oven.

After the company left, Mama heated up more cider. We had corn fritters with maple syrup. Aunt Queen sat next to the hearth, bouncing Star on her knee. Mingo sat on the floor at her feet.

"I can't believe how Corey Birdsong has stretched in his height!" said Aunt Queen. "I can't believe how strong my Mingo is! I can't believe how pretty this cabin be, with those pretty pale-pink curtains!"

Mama smiled at her. "And we can't believe that you are finally here with us, Aunt Queen!"

Aunt Queen chuckled. "Remember the tale of the hare and the tortoise? That tortoise finally gets there."

Daddy laughed.

"Freedom is coming," said Aunt Queen. "It might seem slow, but freedom is coming for everyone. In the end, freedom will be the winner."

Same Day, Later On

I can't sleep. I can't get Aunt Queen's voice out of my head.

Freedom is coming! Tomorrow I am going to tell Aunt Queen how I was a conductor on the Underground Railroad!

I wish that I could go back to the States and be a conductor again. But Mama won't let me work on the *Pearl* anymore. She says that my conducting days are over. After all, I only turned eleven in August.

Maybe I can be a conductor again, when I turn twelve!

November 17, 1859

We have heard tell that Mr. Osborne got away at Harpers Ferry. It is a miracle, Daddy says. Mr. Osborne was with John Brown, but he did not get caught.

Pretty soon, Christmas is coming. I must get busy making my presents.

After Christmas will be the new year —
1860! When will freedom come to all of the
States? Will it be then?

Historical Note

From the time of their arrival in 1619, African slaves helped build America. They were farmers, crafts people, inventors, artists, and healers. Though many slave owners put restrictions on reading and writing, some slaves, like the poet Phillis Wheatley, became writers or scholars. Like many other early Americans, their story is one of accomplishment and survival in the face of great odds. But the history of early African Americans is markedly different, because they came to the American shores in bondage. From the start, they were engaged in a struggle to attain basic personal liberties.

By the time Abraham Lincoln signed the Emancipation Proclamation into law in 1863, slavery had been in existence in parts of North America for more than 240 years! Generations of African-American people lived their whole lives without ever knowing freedom. The story of slavery in America is tragic. But it is also the story of people determined to fight back in order to change their condition.

From their earliest days in America, African Americans resisted slavery in a number of ways. Some, like Nat Turner, led uprisings. Others found ways to escape. Old newspaper articles document the existence of many "runaways." Their escapes were fraught with danger. Many were hunted down and returned to their owners by slave catchers. By the early 1800s, many Americans were firm abolitionists. They spoke out strongly against slavery. Some became part of a secret

John Brown, an abolitionist who led a raid on Harpers Ferry in 1859, found shelter in this carriage house before his capture.

John Brown was tried and hanged for leading a group of abolitionists in the raid on Harpers Ferry.

network that helped fugitives on their way to freedom. This network became known as the Underground Railroad. Black, white, and Native American people banded together to offer the runaways food and hiding places.

The destination for some slaves was a "free" state, such as Ohio or Pennsylvania. But with the passing of the Fugitive Slave Law of 1850, slave catchers were permitted to enter free states in order to hunt the fugitives down and force them back into slavery. So, for many African Americans seeking freedom, the final destination, or "promised land," was Canada.

A ferryboat crossing the river to Amherstburg, Ontario, in Canada.

Map of African-American settlements in Canada
from 1835 to 1870.

Slavery was abolished in Canada in 1793. By
the year 1859, African-Canadian communities
had long been prospering. One of these was in
Amherstburg, Ontario.

Some slave owners in the United States argued that if they freed their slaves, the Africans would not know how to take care of themselves! The history of Amherstburg certainly disproves that argument. In this

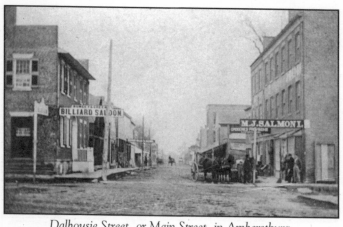

Dalhousie Street, or Main Street, in Amherstburg.

community of former slaves, people of color managed to buy their own farms and start their own businesses. They became teachers and preachers and built their own schools and churches. They were active abolitionists and conductors on the Underground Railroad. When new fugitives escaped across the border, the free black community helped them find work and a place to stay until they got on their feet.

A public schoolhouse in Amherstburg.

Many African-Canadians became known for their outstanding achievements. Mary Ann Shadd Cary started her own newspaper called *The Provincial Freeman*. Dr. Anderson Ruffin Abbott became a surgeon who later returned

African-American farmers working their own land in Amherstburg.

to the States to serve in the Union army. Osborne Anderson joined John Brown in 1859 in his raid on Harpers Ferry and lived to tell about it. Harriet Tubman made her home in Canada, too, making trips back to the States to help rescue fugitives. All these individuals traced their roots to the United States. Though enjoying the benefits of the "promised land" across the border, they continued to work for the freedom of those left behind.

About the Author

Sharon Dennis Wyeth is the author of *Freedom's Wings, Corey's Underground Railroad Diary, Book One,* and Corey's second diary, *Flying Free. Freedom's Wings* was named a Children's Book Council Notable Trade Book in the Field of Social Studies. Ms. Wyeth's other books include *Once on This River* and *A Piece of Heaven,* a New York Public Library Best Book for the Teen Age.

"Writing Corey's diaries has given me such joy. I loved imagining the details of his family's everyday life. I'm sure that once upon a time a real boy like Corey existed — someone brave and observant and fond of nature. . . ."

For my cousin Cory

Acknowledgments

The author wishes to thank the following generous scholars for sharing their knowledge with her: Elise Harding-Davis, curator of the North American Black Historical Museum in Amherstburg, Ontario; Nneka Allen, research assistant; Carl Westmoreland of the National Underground Railroad Freedom Center; and Jennifer Lushear, curator of education at the New Orleans Pharmacy Museum.

The Freedom-Seekers: Blacks in Early Canada, by Daniel G. Hill, published in 1992 by Stoddart Publishing Company, Toronto, was also an invaluable resource.

A special thanks to my editor, Amy Griffin, whose exquisite sensibility I greatly admire.

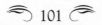

Grateful acknowledgment is made for permission to reprint the following:

Cover portrait by Glenn Harrington.

Page 89 (top): John Brown's fort, CORBIS.

Page 89 (bottom): John Brown's trial, CORBIS.

Page 90: Ferry to Canada, Courtesy of the National Archives of Canada, Ottawa.

Page 91: Map of African-American settlements in Canada, by Jim McMahon.

Page 92: Amherstburg Main Street, Courtesy of the Marsh Collection Society, Amherstburg.

Page 93: Richmond Street Public School, Courtesy of the Park House Museum, Amherstburg.

Page 94: (top): African-American farmers plowing the fields, Courtesy of the Park House Museum, Amherstburg.

Page 94: (bottom): African-American farmers with their equipment, Courtesy of the Buxton National Historic Site and Museum.

Other books in the My America series

Corey's Underground Railroad Diaries
by Sharon Dennis Wyeth
Book One: Freedom's Wings
Book Two: Flying Free

Elizabeth's Jamestown Colony Diaries
by Patricia Hermes
Book One: Our Strange New Land
Book Two: The Starving Time
Book Three: Season of Promise

Hope's Revolutionary War Diaries
by Kristiana Gregory
Book One: Five Smooth Stones
Book Two: We Are Patriots

Joshua's Oregon Trail Diaries
by Patricia Hermes
Book One: Westward to Home
Book Two: A Perfect Place

While the events described and some of the characters in this book
may be based on actual historical events and real people,
Corey Birdsong is a fictional character, created by the author,
and his diary is a work of fiction.

Library of Congress Cataloging-in-Publication Data
Wyeth, Sharon Dennis.
Message in the sky / by Sharon Dennis Wyeth.
p. cm. — (Corey's Underground Railroad diary ; bk. 3)
Summary: Ten-year-old Corey Birdsong, a former slave, becomes a conductor on the
Underground Railroad by helping to bring a mother and daughter, runaway slaves,
to his family's Amherstburg, Ontario, farm in 1859.
ISBN 0-439-37057-4 — ISBN 0-439-37058-2 (pbk.)
1. African Americans — Juvenile fiction. [1. African Americans — Fiction.
2. Fugitive slaves — Fiction. 3. Slavery — Fiction. 4. Underground railroad — Fiction.
5. Homing pigeons — Fiction. 6. Pigeons — Fiction. 7. Amherstburg (Ont.) — Fiction.
8. Canada — History — 1841–1867 — Fiction.] I. Title.
PZ7.W9746 Me 2003
[Fic] — dc21   2002075758

CIP AC

10 9 8 7 6 5 4 3 2 1   03 04 05 06 07

The display type was set in Quercus Hard.
The text type was set in Goudy.
Photo research by Amla Sanghvi
Book design by Elizabeth B. Parisi

Printed in the U.S.A.   23
First edition, May 2003